Take Me Now

A Short Story

CARLY PHILLIPS

Happy Reading!
XO Carly Phillips

Copyright © Karen Drogin 2023
Published by CP Publishing
Print Edition
Cover Photo: Sara Eirew
Cover Design: Cosmic Letterz

* * *

All rights reserved. No part of this book may be reproduced in any form by any means without the prior written consent of the Publisher, excepting brief quotes used in reviews.

This book is a work of fiction. Names, characters, places, and incidents either are products of the author's imagination or are used fictitiously. Any resemblance to actual events or locales or persons, living or dead, is entirely coincidental.

He acts like he barely knows her.
But she knows he's the one.

Matt Banks was ready to tell Harper Sanders that he loved her, that he'd always loved her and that even though they were young, she was his forever girl.

Then her brother stepped in, wanting more for his sister than a garage owner. Too young to stand up for himself, Matt made her brother a promise that he's regretted every day since.

After years of being ignored by the guy she's always loved, Harper is on a dating binge. No one is Matt, but a girl can keep on trying. Then she gets stranded on the side of the road, and she has no choice but to call the only mechanic in town.

Matt comes to her rescue, and then to her bed. It's an idyllic, passion-filled weekend—but there's still the matter of his promise. And a man's word is his bond.

Chapter One

HARPER SANDERS HAD gone on her last date ever. Blind, online, swipe right, introduction by a well-meaning friend, none of the attempts at finding a man she was attracted to worked. None of the dates had accomplished her one and only goal.

Getting Matt Banks out of her head and her heart.

She'd lived in Montlake, Colorado her entire life. She knew everyone and everyone knew her. In fact, she and Matt had grown up together, from preschool through elementary, middle and high school. They'd been friends, too. Good friends, she'd thought, even if she'd been more than a little in love with him. They hung out in school, after school. He knew her likes and dislikes. She'd suffered through him dating other girls and her going out with guys. Neither of them had ever made a move despite the fact that there had been times she believed he might reciprocate her feelings. But she'd held onto hope that one day they'd become adults who acknowledged their feelings.

Then she'd gone away to college, and when she'd

returned home? Matt had been a stranger, one who wanted nothing to do with her. She'd pined for years, but lately, she'd decided to put herself out there with other men. Her best friend getting married had spurred her desire to find true love for herself, too.

Yet despite date after unsuccessful date, nobody lit her fire the way Matt did. It didn't help that she had to see him often, given her coffee shop was located across the street from his garage. That he came into her place often for his coffee. Still, she'd made the attempt to get over him. The large man with his tousled brown hair and sexy blue bedroom eyes that looked at everyone but her.

Last night she'd ended things with what she'd decided was her last attempt at finding a man. Rich Jonas, a new-in-town lawyer had been ... odd to say the least. She'd given him the same three-date minimum she had most of the guys she tried to go out with, hoping that by getting to know them better, she'd find herself interested. But Rich and his too-eager personality had turned her off instead of on.

She'd given him the old 'it's not you it's me' speech. In reality, he just wasn't Matt. And she'd have to see him often, too. Because he, too, came into the coffee shop a lot.

Small towns, she thought, blowing out a puff of air that hovered in a cloud thanks to the freezing temperatures. She let herself into Harper and Em's Bake and Brew, the shop she'd opened with her best friend and a woman Matt had not only dated but actively pursued upon Emily's move to town.

For years now, it was as if Harper didn't exist for him as anything other than a woman he looked right through – unless he was servicing her car, or she was handing him his coffee multiple times a day. Strong, dark, one sugar, she thought, because of course, she had his order memorized. And it frustrated the hell out of her.

"Are you ready to leave on your trip?" Emily asked, greeting her from behind the counter.

Emily always arrived extra early to bake her muffins and cake slices for the morning crowd, leaving her husband, Parker, in their warm bed. He, in turn, took care of their baby daughter, Jillian, until Emily returned home so he could go to his place of business. A babysitter came in later so Emily could work the afternoon shift with Harper. It was the perfect situation, and Harper was envious of her friend's life. She was happy for her, too, but Harper wanted a family of her own.

"Car's packed," she replied. "I'm really looking forward to this weekend."

She was off to Denver for a coffee class in Latte Art, a hands-on experience in foam design. She'd also enrolled in an Alternative Brewing class, which would expose her to different kinds of brewing equipment and their range of "single origins." Learning about farms that specialized in one type of coffee would help her carry more exclusive brands.

Considering the nearby skiing brought in tourists over the winter seeking unique experiences, she knew these classes would help her expand their clientele, even in their tiny town. Emily's dad owned the Ruby Rose Inn, named after his deceased wife / Emily's mom. Recently renovated and expanded, they were advertising far and wide for more upscale customers. Customers who would come into town for Emily's fabulous baked goods and Harper's unique blends of coffee.

Emily smiled. "You deserve some fun. Go, learn new skills, and enjoy." The timer sounded in the kitchen and Emily darted back inside to see to her baked goods.

Harper couldn't hate her willowy blonde friend. She'd gone out with Matt not knowing Harper still had a thing for the man because she'd kept her feelings to herself. And Emily had ended things because of her relationship with her now-husband, who'd been staying at her father's Bed and Breakfast. Emily had also realized that Harper had feelings for Matt, and she'd never knowingly hurt her close friend.

She and Emily couldn't be more different, Harper with her dark hair, wide hips and bigger frame, Emily with her soft blonde hair, lithe body, and beautiful face. But Harper loved her best friend.

"Bye, Em! See you Monday!" Harper called out.

"Bye! Text me!"

The noise of pans and tins falling sounded from the kitchen and Harper laughed as she walked out of the shop and headed to her car parked on the street.

As she opened the door to her car, her gaze drifted across the street where Matt stood in front of the open double garage doors, wiping his hands on what looked like an old greasy rag. When she realized she even found that action sexy, she knew she had a problem.

Jerking her stare away, she climbed into her navy compact car, settling herself in for the three-hour drive. She ran through everything she'd packed, and certain she was set, she put the key in the ignition and turned it on. The car chugged to life, making an unusual sound that she'd never heard before.

Instinct had her looking Matt's way only to see him watching her, a frown on his handsome, bearded face.

"Dammit." She shut the motor off and tried again … and heard the same noise.

Though it made sense to let Matt check things out, checking meant her seeing him, seeing him meant her talking to him, talking to him meant listening to him grunt as if he was merely tolerating what she had to say until he finished his job.

No thank you.

She let the car run for a few long seconds, relieved when the vehicle mellowed out and sounded normal once more. Unable to help herself, she looked across the street again.

Matt had started to walk towards her. Of course, he was worried about her car, she thought. Annoyed by the prospect that it took a motor problem to get him to come to her, she put her vehicle in drive and pulled away, leaving him in the middle of the street, staring at her taillights as she disappeared from view.

She'd barely covered one block when her cell phone rang. She glanced down to see his business name flash on the screen. Although they weren't friends per se, he was the only garage in town, so of course, he had her number.

She answered on speaker. "What?" she asked, knowing she was being rude and her parents had taught her better.

"I don't like the sound of your car, Harper. Why don't you turn around and let me take a look at the engine before you leave for the weekend," Matt said.

She frowned, ignoring the trip of her heart at the sound of her name on his lips. "How do you know I'm going away?"

"Your uncle mentioned it when he was in the shop with his truck." Her retired uncle used to own the hardware store before selling to a man about ten years older than Harper who had moved to the area with his family.

Small town and uncle with loose lips, she thought, her ire building. "I'm on a tight schedule. There's a late lunch with other shop owners I want to make it to."

Matt muttered something to himself and she thought she heard the word stubborn in there. "Then promise you'll call me if you have a problem."

"Yeah, okay. Thanks," she said, softening her tone. It wasn't his fault he didn't reciprocate her feelings.

"Have a good trip," he said in a gruff voice before disconnecting the call.

She'd have a great trip if she could put all these feelings behind her. She couldn't deny his good manners or caring personality. Would she be so crazy for him otherwise? But he didn't *see* her, he never had. And that truth only fed into the insecurities she'd possessed ever since she realized she was bigger than the other girls, and when her curves had developed at an earlier pace and had been much more pronounced than her friends.

She tried not to wonder whether that was why Matt wasn't interested in her, but she'd also dated enough men to know she was a pretty enough woman with a personality they'd enjoyed.

It's not you, it's me. The line she'd used to end more than last night's relationship. And that's what Matt would probably say to her if confronted with the fact that Harper *wanted* him.

She wanted his muscular arms wrapped around her and his full lips coming down hard on hers. She yearned to feel the scratch of his beard on her cheeks and between her thighs. In fact, she desired him to the point where she had full-on erotic dreams starring the man. She wriggled uncomfortably in her seat, her body coming to life at the thought of being with Matt.

But thoughts and dreams were all she'd ever have.

Maybe she'd meet a guy on this trip, she mused, in an attempt to be more optimistic and to lighten her mood. A sexy barista who shared her love of coffee and classic rock and who found her curves the hottest thing he'd ever seen.

And on that hopeful thought, she smiled and put Matt Banks in her rearview mirror, at least for now.

✧ ✧ ✧

"Dammit." Matt Banks slammed his cell phone onto the counter, lucky he didn't break the screen. Harper Sanders drove him mad.

Or maybe he was just mad at himself for the distance he kept between them. Distance he'd *promised* to maintain, and Matt was a man of his word. Not wanting to think about why he stayed away from a woman he desired so badly, he ran a hand through his too-long hair and groaned when the memory of that day stayed with him. Her older brother, Noah, had been home on leave from the Marines, and he'd stopped by Matt's garage that he'd inherited from his late father.

Matt thought Noah had come to ask him to service his jeep that sat in the street while he'd been gone.

Instead, the bulky soldier had stepped into Matt's personal space. "I saw the way you were looking at my sister at the tavern last night."

Matt *had* been eyeing Harper.

He always scoped out the gorgeous full-figured woman he'd been in love with forever. But they'd grown up together as friends. They'd been young. Neither made a move. Then she'd gone to college and he'd waited, knowing she'd be home for good one day, and he'd planned to act then. That time had come, and he'd been considering how he was going to ask her out, but she'd left with her friends before he could do it.

"So?" He stood up to her brother.

"So she can do better than a garage owner without an education, that's what. And since I'm not around to make sure you keep your hands to yourself, I want your word you'll leave my sister alone," Noah said, his fists clenched as he made his point.

In doing so, Noah had hit at the sore spot Matt never admitted to the world. His father died and he'd taken over the garage, giving up any dreams he'd had of higher education or being more than a guy who worked with his hands for a living. Over time, he realized he found running the business fulfilling, working on cars soothing to his peace of mind.

But at the time? With the bigger man looming over him and Matt's own insecurities new and in full force? Knowing that like him, Harper had lost her father only when she was much younger, her brother was like her male parent and role model. And he'd pointed out shortcomings in Matt he'd thought about himself.

So he'd caved. "Yeah. Right. Whatever," he'd muttered. "I'll leave her alone."

And he had.

Because his own father, someone he admired with all his heart and soul, had taught him a man's word was his bond. He'd watched Harper from afar, and it was fucking pathetic. Especially lately, as she'd dated man after man, Matt wishing he could step up and claim her as his own. He wasn't one to talk. He'd dated her best friend. Hell, he'd really pursued her, all in a misguided effort to get over Harper.

He shook his head and his thoughts returned to

more pressing matters. The sound her car had made as she drove out of town. He hoped like hell that noise wasn't what he thought it was, or her serpentine belt was either going to break or already had. Which meant the car was destined to overheat, causing damage to the alternator, the radiator, and the steering pump, among other things. Which didn't make sense since he'd inspected her car last month and it had passed.

If it wouldn't make him seem like a stalker, he'd jump into his truck and follow her route now. But he wasn't one hundred percent certain where she was headed nor did he think she'd appreciate the tail. Which meant he'd better get busy finishing up his work for this afternoon because he fully expected a phone call when her car died and she ended up on the side of the road.

Sure enough, the call came an hour later, and due to the grateful tone in Harper's voice, he couldn't bring himself to say *I told you so*.

Instead, he closed up shop, stopped by his place to pick up a few things, and headed towards Denver. The word 'opportunity' had been floating through his head all day as he'd waited for her call. He'd made a promise to her brother when he was little more than a kid who merely thought he was an adult. A twenty-two-year-old forced to grow up fast but who hadn't had enough experience to stand up for himself as a man.

Matt had that experience now. He was a fully-grown man who knew what he wanted, what he deserved, and more importantly, what he could give to Harper. Even his father would forgive him for breaking this promise because Roger Banks had believed in true love. Although Harper's brother, who had retired from the Marines, now ran a gun shop in town, and would probably want to use one of those weapons on Matt after he defied him, Matt didn't care.

Fuck it. No Marine, regardless of the fact that he was Harper's brother, was going to keep Matt from Harper any longer. The only obstacle to being with the woman he loved? Was that woman herself.

Chapter Two

HARPER HATED HER stubbornness. She hated that Matt was right. And most of all, she hated that she'd had to call on him to rescue her. Sitting on the side of the road, her gloves on her hands, scarf around her neck, her jacket zipped up tight, she shivered, waiting for him to arrive and rescue her.

She had too much time to think about the weekend she was now going to miss, how she'd really been looking forward to learning new foam techniques and making pretty hearts and squiggles in her customer's cups. Not to mention a weekend to herself in Denver, no work, nothing to do but enjoy. Now she'd have to drive home in Matt's tow truck with him muttering about how she could have saved them both the trouble by letting him check out her car before she left town.

Expecting it to take at least an hour for him to arrive, she was shocked when he showed up forty-five minutes later, skidding to a stop behind her car in his Tahoe and not his tow truck.

She opened her door just as he walked up to her side of the car. He wore his heavy parka. Her toes were frozen, her body almost numb. Just seeing him, his handsome face, and the worry in his brown eyes made her want to cry in relief.

"Did you fly here?" she asked, half-jokingly.

He looked down at her and a semi-smile lifted his sexy mouth. "No. Now, go get in my warm truck. Let me see what's going on with your car."

Unwilling to argue after hearing the word *warm*, she rushed to his vehicle, climbed into the passenger seat and slammed her door shut. The inside smelled like musky man, like Matt, and she breathed in deep, savoring the scent before she whipped off her gloves and held her hands up to the hot air blowing from the vents.

As she warmed herself, she watched as Matt first popped the hood and inspected the engine, then slammed it shut, a scowl on his face. From there, he opened her trunk and loaded her luggage into the back of his truck before returning to the driver's side.

"Hey," he said, as he slid into his seat. "So your belt is broken, which is what I thought that sound was. Good thing you pulled over before the engine overheated."

Even his frown was sexy, she thought to herself. "Why didn't you bring your tow truck?"

He slung an arm over the top of the seats and turned towards her. "Because I know how much this weekend and these classes mean to you, so we're going to Denver. I'll call someone to tow the car to the garage when we get there."

She blinked in surprise. "I'm sorry... what? You're not taking me back home?"

"No."

"But –"

He rolled his eyes at her. "You're going to argue with me when you're getting exactly what you want?"

"No," she whispered. But why was he being so... so... chivalrous? And nice? "How do you know about my classes? Never mind, my uncle," she said, answering her own question.

He chuckled and gave her a nod. Turning in his seat, he started the car and headed toward her original destination.

"What about the garage?" she asked, knowing he worked long hours, and though he had employees, he liked to be there himself.

He glanced from her back to the road. "Harry can handle things for the weekend."

Just... wow. "Matt?"

"Yes?" One hand on the wheel, he glanced over at her. He'd put on sunglasses that covered his eyes, and she drank in the sight of him.

She swallowed hard. "Thank you for coming to get me. And for taking me to Denver." She couldn't believe that was his plan.

"You're welcome," he said in a gruff voice. "What hotel are you staying in?"

She rubbed her hands together, pleased they were finally warm. Even her feet felt better, the heat from beneath the dashboard doing its job. "The Four Seasons, where the class is being held."

He let out a low whistle. "Nice."

"Another reason I was looking forward to the weekend," she admitted. "Can't beat the luxuries there."

"I'll bet."

A quiet few moments passed, and she squirmed in her seat, struggling to find some subject with which to make conversation when he surprised her.

"So, tell me about these classes you're taking."

She raised an eyebrow. "You cannot be interested in coffee-making classes."

"I'm asking, aren't I? It interests you, so I'm curious. Tell me," he insisted.

She slid her tongue over her bottom lip, shocked when she glanced at him to realize he'd been sneaking a look at her, watching the movement.

"Umm ... first, there's the foam-making class." For the next half hour, she told him in detail about each session she was scheduled to attend, and he asked questions that indicated interest.

Not just 'pass the time' interest but true attentiveness. Like what she said mattered. By the time they arrived in Denver, they'd had their first real conversation about various things they each enjoyed … in forever.

"What kind of music do you like?" he asked.

"Classic rock. If the station holds while we drive, I like 105."

With a grin, he flipped on the radio, and she discovered her favorite station was set and ready to play.

Over the course of the drive, she learned some other things, too. It was one thing to think she was in love with the man because she liked his looks and appreciated the decent man he was on the inside … despite his usual surliness towards her. Quite another to have common interests.

Matt Banks shared her love of Queen, The Who, and Guns n' Roses among other artists. She often thought she belonged in another generation. But Matt understood her appreciation of the albums from another era. And it turned out he really loved her coffee, something he admitted to her as they pulled into the front of the hotel for valet parking.

By the time they strode up to the front desk for check-in, her feelings had gone from the abstract to the tangible. Which meant she needed her space from him, and she needed it now.

She handed the front desk her license and credit card. "I'm booked through the weekend," she said. "Harper Sanders."

The middle-aged clerk clicked his computer keys and nodded. "Yes. You have a king bed, Ms. Sanders."

"Thank you. I'll need an extra room for my ... friend. He came with me unexpectedly." And she intended to pay for his room whether he liked it or not. No matter how big a dent it put in her credit card. Her room had come with the coffee class discount.

She felt the heat of Matt's big body behind her, his tall frame looming over hers. There weren't many men who could make Harper feel small, but Matt accomplished that feat.

The man behind the desk clicked away at his keyboard, a frown on his face, and Harper's stomach twisted with worry. "What's wrong?"

"I'm sorry, but we're booked. We have a few conventions here this weekend. There are no extra rooms." He glanced up, an apologetic look on his face.

"But – Do you have a room with two double beds?" She grasped for the next best thing.

Not ideal, considering she had no idea how she was going to share a room with Matt when all she wanted to do was climb his big body and attach herself to him. Naked.

The clerk shook his head. "No, ma'am. Again, I'm sorry."

"But –"

Matt placed a calming hand on her shoulder, coming up beside her. "It's fine. We'll take the room you have and make do," he said to the clerk, who was looking back and forth between them.

Make do.

She glanced at him, and her stomach plummeted at his words, a stark reminder that just because he was doing her a favor, she had no business conjuring visions of them together.

Erotic visions, no less.

✧ ✧ ✧

SHARING A ROOM?

That worked for him.

Of course, he'd put his foot in his mouth, too.

Matt took one look at Harper's face and wanted to kick himself for his poor choice of words. It wasn't how he'd meant it … but he'd said it. Now he had to make it up to her.

He took the keys from the desk clerk and thanked him before turning to Harper. "Come on. I can carry our luggage up." They each had one small rolling piece and he'd have no trouble with them both. As soon as he realized he'd be rescuing her, he'd decided he was taking her to Denver for the weekend and staying overnight, hence his trip to his place before hitting the road.

They took the elevator to the sixth floor in silence, and though that had been their M.O., the car ride and her happy chatter had spoiled him for more than stiff, cordial interactions.

Stopping at the door of their room, he pulled the key from his jacket pocket and let them inside. The door shut behind them, enclosing them in an elegant, gorgeous space. He took in the large white bed in the center, knowing exactly what he wanted to be doing in the middle of it. The sun shone over the dark wood furniture, and a large television sat on the credenza. This was beyond his means normally, and he assumed Harper had gotten a conference rate. They might as well enjoy it.

He took off his jacket and placed it over the chair, noticing she'd removed hers and hung it in the closet.

Uncomfortable silence echoed around them until she broke it. "I missed the lunch, but I'm hungry so I'm going to go downstairs and –"

"Harper, wait." She turned.

He took in her gorgeous face, not happy at the moment but no less beautiful, the curvy body in a pair of black pants and a light pink blouse that accentuated her lush, full breasts, and he broke.

He strode to her, cupped her face in his hand, pulled her towards him, and sealed his lips over hers. She raised her hands to his shoulders, and he mentally prepared for her to shove him away. Instead, she curled her fingers into his shirt and clung to him as her mouth parted and she let him in.

Their tongues met, teeth clashed, the kiss was hard and needy, and so many years in the making. He wanted to take his time and savor the moment, but he couldn't. Not when he thought she was right there with him.

But she wasn't because she pulled back, her gaze meeting his. "You do realize we have things to discuss," she informed him haughtily.

"Yeah," he muttered, nudging his dick at her entrance. "But can't it wait?"

She hesitated, giving his question careful consideration before nodding. "Yes. But you're not getting out of talking."

"Wouldn't dream of it," he promised.

Obviously assured, she pulled his shirt from the waistband of his pants, and they separated long enough to take a breath and for him to throw his shirt to the floor.

He kissed her again while bringing his hands to the buttons on her shirt, but his hands were too big, and he fumbled with them.

"Fuck it," he muttered and pulled at the sides, sending buttons flying everywhere.

She gasped but didn't seem to mind as she merely shrugged the blouse off her shoulders and let it glide to the floor. And what he saw, he'd only dreamed of until now. Her large breasts strained the fabric tipped in lace, creamy soft mounds of flesh plumping over the edges.

He met her gaze, shocked to find uncertainty in her blue eyes, and he couldn't have that between them. "So beautiful." He followed the scalloped border with one finger, his breath coming in uneven pants.

She splayed her hands on his chest, running her fingers over his skin, setting his body aflame. He kissed her again, devouring her, gliding his mouth back and forth over hers. They were in sync, every moment perfect and more than he'd imagined. And he'd done that plenty, jerking off to visions of Harper as he came.

"Pants," she said, breaking the kiss. "I want them off. I need to see you. Touch you. I need to know this is real."

"It's as real as it gets," he assured her.

But he wanted the same thing she did, so he stepped back and undid his jeans, yanking them down along with his boxer briefs, aware that she was doing the same, ridding herself of the remainder of her clothing.

Once freed, his cock sprung upright against his abdomen, desire pulsing through his veins. And when he caught sight of her body, creamy white flesh, delicious curves, all his dreams come to life, it pulsed once more.

He stepped toward her, and she backed up, falling against the mattress with a soft laugh. She pushed herself back to the mound of pillows and he followed, coming over her, wanting nothing more than to thrust hard and deep into her slick, waiting sex.

"I'm not going to last long this first time," he told her.

She lifted her eyebrows in a way he found both enticing and adorable. "First time?"

"You don't dream about something as long as I've dreamt of you and get your fill in one shot."

"Good to know," she said with a sexy smile, writhing as he positioned himself, the head of his cock poised and ready.

Until he realized one important thing. "Condom." He jumped up, grabbing his jeans and retrieving one from his pocket.

"Men," she said, rolling her eyes. "Always prepared."

"It's older than dirt," he informed her. "But not

that old that it won't work. Oh, shit." He just kept putting his foot in his mouth.

She shook her head and laughed. "Never mind. I get it. Just hurry up!"

He returned, his cock once again at the entrance of her sex, and immediately pushed in … slowly because he knew he was a big man with a big dick … and he felt himself stretching her tight inner walls.

God, had anything ever felt so good? So perfect?

"Faster, Matt, please."

"I don't want to hurt you."

She pinched his shoulder. "Move or I'll hurt *you*."

She'd released him from the constraints restraining him, and he was barely holding on as it was. He began to move in and out, taking her hard and fast, and she accepted him, having no trouble with his pace or how hard he thrust into her. She arched her back, pulling him deeper, and he saw stars, then she wrapped her legs around his waist until their bodies practically joined.

Jesus, she was killing him, and he loved every minute.

Bracing his hands on the bed, he raised himself enough to rock and grind into her, their bodies in complete unison. He rolled his hips and she started to shake, her hands pulling at his hair.

"Oh, God, Matt, yes. Keep going."

He ground into her, and suddenly she moaned, low and deep, writhing in his arms. Her climax set off his own, and he thrust into her again and again, knowing this was what had been missing from his life for so long.

Chapter Three

Harper lay in Matt's arms, completely satisfied if not still stunned that she'd ended up in bed with the man she'd never been able to get out of her heart.

"I can hear the wheels turning," Matt said, his hands stroking her arm. "What's wrong?"

She had to ask because she had to know. "Why did we get together now? Or should I say what held you back until now?" She bit down on her lower lip after questioning him.

He stiffened but didn't speak, and in the wake of his silence, she couldn't help what came out of her mouth next. "I always wondered if it was me. My curves. My body."

"Fuck, no!" He pulled himself up and over her so she was looking into his face, his expression pained. "I always wanted you," he assured her. "These curves. This body." He slid his hand over her waist and around her hips. "But ..." He drew a deep breath. "I made a promise to your brother that I'd leave you alone."

"What?" She couldn't have heard what she thought she did. "Noah?"

Matt nodded somberly.

"He didn't," she said on an angry growl. "He meddled in my life?"

"He did, but he was looking out for you. He was doing what your father couldn't," Matt said. "Besides, I'm the one at fault ... for listening to him." Matt appeared both sad and ashamed. "The things he said, they hit a nerve. That you deserved someone better, smarter, with a college education."

She could see how hard it was for him to admit to what he and her asshole brother considered shortcomings.

"Well, Noah had no right to get involved. And I see you as someone bright enough to take over a business at too young an age and make sure it thrived. You're smart enough to fix any car brought into your shop. You have a big heart and an even bigger ..."

"Hey." He tickled her sides and she writhed with laughter.

As she sobered, she asked, "What made you change your mind?"

He met her gaze. "I knew you were going to call me when the belt broke on the car. And all I could think about was how this was my chance. I wasn't going to let you miss classes that meant so much to you, so I was going to take you to Denver. We were going to be together. I could go after what I wanted or regret it for the rest of my life."

She blinked back tears. "Well, I'm glad you did."

He kissed her, and she sighed into him. His hands skimmed over her sides, coming up to her breasts, pausing as he fondled her, cupping them in his big hand.

He lifted his head, his gaze coming to rest on her breasts.

"What?" she asked.

He lifted each globe in one of his big hands. "I've always thought about you. Jerked off to the idea of thrusting in between these fabulous breasts." Leaning down, he licked at first one nipple, then the next.

She didn't know if it was an attempt to distract her, but she couldn't stop thinking about what he said even as her sex swelled and she grew damp while he sucked and nipped at the tight buds.

She drew a deep breath and said, "Try it."

"What?"

"Play out your fantasy." She lifted her breasts and offered them to him.

His blue eyes darkened to nearly black. "Yeah?"

"Yeah." There wasn't much she wouldn't do with this man.

He leaned down and kissed her, slowly and leisurely, rolling his tongue against hers, telling her without words what her offer meant to him. Then he raised his head and slid forward until his thick, hard cock rested between her cleavage.

"Hold your breasts tighter in your hands," he said in a rough voice she felt straight down to her clit.

She watched his face, the play of emotions in his expression as his gaze came to rest on her breasts once more. She did as he asked, gripping herself with both hands. It felt odd, touching herself in front of him.

"Now squeeze them together."

As she pushed her breasts, she captured his cock between the two mounds of flesh. Leaning forward, he began thrusting his cock, tunneling in and out of the cavern she'd created.

As she watched his taut expression and felt him pass through her breasts, she found herself getting more aroused. It was sexy as hell, him getting off this way.

His rhythm started out slow and sure, but the closer to orgasm, the jerkier his movements. And his grunts and groans grew louder until suddenly he stiffened, streams of pearly liquid spreading over her chest as he came. And he continued to come until he collapsed into a sitting position, his breathing coming in shallow spurts.

"That was better than any fucking fantasy." Picking her up, he carried her into the bathroom.

They showered, cleaning off only to have him drop to his knees so he could lick, suck and play with her sex until bright lights flickered behind her eyes and she came so hard she would have fallen had he not been there to support her.

An hour later, they shared room service only to end up back in bed where they enjoyed each other some more before falling asleep in sated heaps.

The next morning, they woke up late, having forgotten to set an alarm, and Harper rushed to get ready for her first class. She still had to figure out where in the hotel the session was being held and eat something so she didn't pass out during the long hours ahead of her.

But through her quick shower and putting on her makeup, she practically bounced on the balls of her feet, happy in a way she'd never been.

Yet in the back of her mind was the niggling thought that so much time had been wasted and it was so unfair. But they'd found each other now, and she wasn't going to dwell on what she couldn't change. Except she was going to kick her brother's ass when she got home.

✧ ✧ ✧

MATT LISTENED TO Harper humming in the bathroom as she got ready for class. A lead weight sat in his stomach. Not because he regretted anything with Harper last night, but because he was worried about her car, which led to concern about *her*.

Last night he'd been preoccupied with finally having her in his arms, and besides, there hadn't been anything he could have done that late. But her serpentine belt had been tampered with. Someone had deliberately sabotaged her car. Not wanting to upset her or ruin her weekend, he didn't mention the issue.

He picked up his phone and called Harry. "Hey man, can you have a tow sent for Harper's car?" He gave his worker the mile marker and the road name where he'd left the vehicle. "When you get it back to the shop, check it out top to bottom, but pay special attention to the belt. I think someone played with it."

"Sure thing, Boss."

"See you Monday." The shop was closed on Sunday and Harry had the day off.

"Ready!" Harper joined him in the room.

He smiled at the sight of her, pretty in her black slacks and white shirt, her hair pulled back in a ponytail. "I'll see you to class then go exploring," he told her.

"Sounds good."

They left the room and walked down the hall hand

in hand. He'd never expected to be with Harper, never mind have it feel so perfect or right. God, he was head over heels for this woman.

At the ballroom where her class was being held, he kissed her long and hard before leaving her for the day.

Then he headed into town with the intention of doing some very specific shopping for one extremely special woman. Afterward, he killed time until he had to meet up with Harper, preoccupied with thoughts of her. How much he loved her despite the fact that they'd only been together one night. Despite that, they had a lot of time to make up for and things to learn about each other.

But before he laid his heart out to her, he needed to stand up to her brother and hopefully get his approval. Only then could he come to her and ask her for forever.

✧ ✧ ✧

THE FULL-DAY CLASS ended early, and Harper sat at a table inside the lobby lounge, ironically drinking coffee. Susie Majors, a friendly barista Harper had met early in the day, joined her.

"So, where are you from and where do you work?" Harper asked the pretty brunette, although Harper had a hunch about what part of the country from which the woman originated.

"I'm from Tennessee." Susie laughed. "Did the accent give me away?"

Harper chuckled. "Only a little."

"Anyway, I work at a Starbucks in downtown Denver now, but I'm hoping to open my own place one day. I'm taking all the classes I can so I'm prepared if and when that time comes." Susie took a long sip of the hotel brew.

Harper smiled. "Well, if you ever need advice or pointers, I've done it... twice. Once with my own shop and once on a full renovation when my best friend and I turned the combined space into a bakery and coffee shop." She handed her a business card. "Keep in touch."

"I will." Susie slid her own card across the table and Harper pocketed it, feeling like she'd connected with her and made a friend.

She and Susie were talking about what they'd learned today when the other woman's eyes opened wide. "Oh, wow. They don't make men like that where I come from," Susie said in an appreciative tone of voice, fake fanning herself with her hand.

Harper grabbed the back of her chair and turned to see Matt striding towards them, an intense feeling of possessiveness filling her as she looked over the handsome man, from his bearded face – a beard which she'd indeed felt against her thighs late last night – to his bulky body.

Before she could pivot back to Susie, Matt reached her, leaned down, and pressed his lips to hers. The kiss was long and equally as possessive as she'd felt towards him. By the time she turned around, her cheeks were flaming as she met Susie's startled gaze.

"Oh! I didn't realize he was yours," the other woman said, clearly flustered.

Was he hers? Harper wondered. Or was this a weekend outside of their normal routine and he'd go back to ignoring her when they returned to Montlake? As much as she wanted to know, she wouldn't ask and ruin their time together. She'd find out where they stood soon enough. They were going home tomorrow.

"I'm Matt," he said, extending his hand to Susie to shake.

"I'm Susie."

"Nice to meet you, Susie." Matt looked down at Harper. "Are you all finished?"

She nodded, rising from her chair. "Save me a seat tomorrow if you get there first?" she asked Susie.

Her class was an hour in the morning and then they could start their trip home.

"I will. And you do the same." Susie rose and threw her cup in the trash. "See you tomorrow!" She strode out into the lobby.

Matt turned to Harper. "Did you have a good day?"

"I did. It was so much fun, and I learned amazing techniques."

"I'm glad." He grasped her hand and led her to the elevator. "I'm also glad we have one more night here," he said as they stepped into the lift.

Once the doors closed, he backed her against the wall and pressed his mouth against hers. His tongue swirled around the deep recesses of her mouth and she moaned, rubbing her breasts against his chest.

He broke contact long enough to look into her eyes and touch his nose to hers. "I missed you." He dipped his head once more to continue the kiss, but the elevator dinged, announcing they'd come to their floor.

He took her hand and led her to their room, opening the door and letting them inside. She kicked off her shoes and walked into the room, stopping short when she saw an ice bucket with champagne and chocolate-covered strawberries on a plate.

"Matt?" She spun to face him.

"I just wanted to do something nice for you." He lifted the bottle out of the ice, untwisted the wire covering and popped the cork. "I have dinner coming up in half an hour. I thought you'd be tired after a full day of classes."

Even as her stomach growled at the thought of food, her eyes misted, and though she felt silly, she couldn't help it. No one had ever done anything so sweet for her before. She never thought she'd have this caring man in her life. And she didn't want to lose him. That was the thought behind the tears, but she wasn't ready to express her fears.

Instead, she stepped over and accepted the glass of champagne he'd poured for her and took a sip. The bubbles tickled her throat. "Mmm."

His sexy grin aroused her and she forgot all about being hungry. Well, hungry for anything but him, that is. "How about a quickie before we eat?"

He picked her up and tossed her onto the bed. Laughing, they rolled over and stripped each other out of their clothes, coming together in the center of the mattress. Their bodies aligned, his hard cock pressing against her belly.

She moaned and he rolled onto his back, easing her on top of him. "Condom," he reminded her. "I picked some up this afternoon." He gestured to the bag on the counter.

She leaned over pulled one out, handing it to him so he could cover himself. His gaze came to rest on hers. "Ride me, beautiful."

She pushed herself to a sitting position, coming astride him, her core settling over his erection. She gripped his shaft and lowered herself onto him, feeling him fill her up completely.

She groaned loudly, the sound coming from deep inside her. She felt so much for him and wanted to tell him. She needed to say the words, but she didn't know if he reciprocated or if in his mind this was pure desire, not love. But she also understood this was new and they had a lot to learn about each other. So she cautioned herself to take things slow and appreciate what they had now.

Then he reached out and slid his finger over her clit, causing delicious tremors to shoot through her body. She trembled, emotion and sensation building along with the waves of need that threatened to consume her. He thrust his hips up over and over, rising to meet her, causing her breasts to bounce as she rode him.

Her climax hit suddenly and she cried out, calling his name. He gripped her hips hard and came at the same time, his big body shuddering beneath her.

For the rest of the night, they snuggled in bed, rising only to eat. They talked. A lot. She learned more about his life, realizing that he was as lonely as she'd been.

"I'd watch you, you know, as I worked."

"You did?"

"Mmm-hmm. And how do you think I learned to

love coffee so damn much?" he asked, sitting up in bed, holding her in the crook of his arm.

She laughed. "I just thought you liked to torment me." She was only half-joking. Because he had come into the shop often, but given he worked across the street, it seemed normal. "I watched you, too," she murmured.

He grunted at that as if it was hard for him to believe. "You dated a lot," he said gruffly, taking her off guard. "Especially lately."

She sighed and lay her head against him. "I was trying to get over you," she admitted. "Emily getting married really forced me to face that I needed to move on with my life."

"I thought I was doing what was best by staying far away." He leaned down and kissed her.

"And now?" she asked, holding her breath, hoping he'd give her the answer she needed.

"Now we make up for lost time." And for the rest of the night, he proceeded to do just that.

Chapter Four

THE WEEKEND WITH Harper flew by, and before Matt knew it, he was back in his hometown. Since he opened his garage earlier than most businesses, he couldn't stop by the gun shop to see Noah Sanders. He'd have to go by during lunch, which meant he had to wait before showing any public display of affection with Harper. He didn't want rumors to get back to her brother before Matt talked to him face-to-face. He hated staying away, but his word still meant something, as did his respect for the man in the uniform who'd only been looking out for his sister.

Matt worked a long day, with customer after customer coming in with emergencies. He never got a chance to run out and head over to Noah's to talk. All the while, he knew Harper was across the street serving coffee and testing out her new foam techniques and wanting nothing more than to show up and see for himself. But if he saw her, he'd want to touch her, kiss her, drag her into a back room and fuck her senseless then make love to her slowly so she'd know exactly how he felt about her.

Instead, he spent hours in the bay, drinking the swill from a shitty coffee maker rather than the amazing brew Harper created across the street.

Late in the afternoon, he looked outside, hoping for a glimpse of Harper when he caught sight of someone circling her vehicle in Matt's parking lot alongside the garage. He'd had to order a new belt and she wouldn't be driving it until the car was fixed.

So what would a guy be doing lurking by Harper's car?

Wiping his hands on the rag he always kept in his back pocket, Matt headed outside to confront the man. He didn't even stop to grab a coat.

Wearing a black down jacket and a scarf wrapped so it covered half his face, the man stalked Harper's vehicle, muttering out loud as he walked around.

"Hey." Matt stopped the man and shoved him against the window. "What do you think you're doing?"

"I –"

Matt pulled at the scarf, revealing his face. He recognized Rich Jonas as the new lawyer in town who Harper had been dating. "What the fuck?" Matt asked.

"Matt? Rich?" Harper's voice startled Matt and he turned to face her. "What's going on?" she asked.

Matt glanced from her face – her nose had already turned red from the bitter cold – to Rich. "Ask him. I caught him skulking around your car."

She wrapped her arms around her chest, pushing those full breasts up and revealing more than a hint of her cleavage. He'd tasted that skin and wanted more. His dick perked up at the thought. Too bad now wasn't the time.

"Rich?" she asked, sounding confused.

He mumbled something unintelligible, obviously not wanting to admit to whatever he'd been doing.

"Speak up," Matt ordered the man.

"I just thought if I caused some trouble with her car, she'd need someone to rely on and she'd ask me for help."

She blinked in disbelief. "Seriously? Are you that desperate? I was on a highway when the car started to give out! I could have been killed!"

Rich held up both hands in defeat. "I'm sorry! I thought you'd drive it around town … that you'd stall. I didn't think –"

Matt's anger grew as he listened to the man's explanation, and he grabbed him by the jacket and yanked him up so they were nose to nose. "I swear to God, if I catch you around Harper or her car again, you'll wish you never set foot in this town. And if you pull this shit with another woman, I'm going to the cops. Now get the fuck out of here."

Eyes wide, the other man nodded. "Going. I'm going." He didn't even look at Harper before running out of the lot and not looking back.

Matt took one look at his girl with her chattering teeth and wide eyes, wrapped his arms around her, and led her into the garage. He had a space heater running in the small office, and he slammed the door shut so she could warm up.

Pulling her against him, he enfolded her in his body heat, and she cuddled into him, where she belonged.

✧ ✧ ✧

Harper waited until she warmed up, taking advantage of Matt's big body and grabbing a few precious minutes in his arms before shoving him away. "Where the hell have you been all day?"

They both came in to work early, and he always, always came by the second she opened for his first cup of coffee for the day. And that was before they'd been intimate. Today, their first day back, he'd been conspicuously absent from her shop, and she refused to go back to the way things were between them. Not without a good explanation.

"I had a crazy busy day and ... Fuck."

She narrowed her gaze.

He looked her in the eyes and sealed his lips over hers, kissing her long and hard until she was out of breath. When he broke the kiss, he had a determined look in his eyes. "Let's go."

"Where?" she asked, perplexed and off-kilter from his behavior.

"To see your brother." He grabbed his jacket off a hook and wrapped it around her shoulders before grasping her hand and leading her to his Tahoe.

"Why?" she asked once they were on their way. "I told you I'd handle him."

He shook his head. One hand on the wheel, he glanced over at her. "This is my fight."

"Okay." From his curt tone of voice, she wasn't about to argue.

They arrived at the gun shop, and Matt parked then came around and helped her out of the truck. "Any chance you'll wait for me here?"

She tipped her head to the side. "Really? Umm, no."

He set his jaw, grabbed her hand, and together they walked across the lot and into her brother's store. Noah was alone, no customers in sight, for which Harper was grateful. She didn't know what was about to happen between the men, but she didn't want an audience.

"Harper? Matt?" Noah, with his Marine-style

cropped hair and big body, would intimidate most men.

And Harper could see how he'd have pushed a younger Matt around. But the man by her side now? He was strong and proud, and she was equally proud of him as he strode up to her brother.

"Noah. About that promise I made you to stay away from your sister? I'm breaking it. I love her, and she loves me –"

A heady warmth settled inside of Harper at his words. Words they'd yet to exchange to each other, but she understood this promise had prevented them from moving forward.

"Look," Noah began.

Matt shook his head. "I'm not finished. I love her, and I'm good enough for her. I might not have understood that when I was younger, but I do now. So, though I'd like your approval, I'm letting you know you're not going to stand in our way."

Harper wasn't going to let him stop her from having the man of her dreams either, but right now, the two men faced off in a tense, silent battle of wills.

To her utter shock, Noah took a step forward and extended his hand to Matt. "All I ever wanted for my sister was a man who knew his own worth," Noah said.

Harper narrowed her gaze. "You jerk! Do you

have any idea how much you screwed up my life? How much all these years of him ignoring me *hurt* me?"

She was about to dive over the counter and attempt to beat up her brother like she did when they were kids, but Matt grabbed her around the waist.

"He loves you, Harper. He wanted someone who could love and provide for you. Who'd put you first. I can't fault him for that. But if he gets in our way again? I'll jump over that counter and go after him myself. Okay?" Matt asked her.

Harper's heart beat hard in her chest. It wasn't enough. Not nearly enough after the pain she'd endured thinking Matt didn't want her. But if he could forgive her brother for acting like an overbearing jerk, she'd try and do the same.

"Fine," she muttered, glaring at Noah who at least looked ashamed, his hand still extended for Matt to take.

Matt, who'd waited for her to agree before gripping Noah's hand in a rough man-to-man shake.

"Harp, I'm sorry," her brother said, coming around the counter. "I just thought ... he was just taking over the garage. I saw how you two looked at each other, and I wanted to make sure he succeeded before you two hooked up and maybe you got dragged down. I was ... I shouldn't have gotten involved."

Which was a big *I'm sorry* from the Marine.

"No, you shouldn't have."

"Forgive me?" Noah asked.

She frowned, but he was her family. Her blood. Her mom would be so hurt if her kids were at war. "Fine. But promise me, never again."

His eyes lit up at her words. "I promise."

"Then okay. I guess I forgive you."

Her brother pulled her into a hug.

As she stepped out of his embrace, she turned to tell Matt they could go ... and he was kneeling. Seriously, down on one knee, a jewelry box open in his hand, a beautiful, round diamond ring sparkling at her.

Her mouth opened wide and closed.

"Now that that's out of the way, Harper Sanders, will you marry me?" Matt asked, that sexy gaze holding onto hers.

She swallowed hard. "I ... but we just got together. We need time to –"

"Get to know each other?" Matt let out a laugh. "We've known each other forever, and we have a lifetime to learn everything we don't know. Haven't we wasted enough time?"

"Yes." She blurted the word, having no need to think things through. This was the man she'd dreamed of having. The man she wanted to have a future with. Children with. "Yes!"

He slipped the ring onto her finger and then she

was in his arms, tears dripping down her face as she glanced up and saw her brother looking at them, a pleased expression on his face.

Chapter Five

Harper took the steamed milk and poured it gradually into the Espresso, starting in the middle, holding the pitcher high so the poured milk would sink to the bottom. When the cup was mostly full, she continued to pour but this time closer to the top, shaking her hand back and forth to make ripples in the foam. As her last step, she lifted her pour higher again and dragged a line through the center of the heart to make a point at the bottom.

And voila. A perfect heart-shaped foam in her cappuccino.

Her ring twinkled as she worked, and she grinned. Every time she looked down at her hand, she smiled, unable to believe the difference between today … and just last week. And all it had taken was one disgruntled ex-date to fiddle with the belt on her car and force Matt to take a hard look at his life without her in it.

"Somebody looks happy," Emily said as she came out from the kitchen, rubbing her hands on her apron.

"Somebody is happy." Harper held out her hand

for her best friend's inspection.

Emily screamed. "You're engaged! Oh, my God! I know you told me you finally got together with Matt in Denver but ... oh, my God!" She picked up Harper's hand and smiled. "I am so happy for you, my friend. Nobody, and I mean nobody deserves this more than you."

After a long hug that squeezed the breath out of her lungs, Harper pulled back. "I love you, Em. You're a great friend."

"Back at you."

The bell rang over the door, and they both turned at the same time. "Matt!" Emily exclaimed, running over and giving Harper's man a tight squeeze, too. "Congratulations!"

"Thanks." A red flush highlighted his cheekbones above his beard. "Can I steal my girl?"

It was Harper's turn to blush at his words. Words she'd never get tired of hearing.

"Sure!" Emily headed back into the kitchen.

"What's up?" Harper asked him.

He looked around the shop. "You have someone covering the counter?"

She nodded. "We're good. What did you need?"

His eyes darkened as they raked over her body. "You. Now that we're a couple and I can see you whenever I want, I can't get enough," he said in a growly voice that hit her low in her abdomen.

"Come with me." She grasped his hand and led him across the store to where her private office was located, her pulse picking up with every step.

They made it into the office, and he slammed the door shut and locked it behind them.

Matt immediately lifted her up and into his arms. She wrapped her legs around his waist and her arms around his neck, holding on as he slid his mouth over hers. His tongue plunged in deep and he devoured her as if he needed her to breathe. Harper had never been desired this way before or needed so much, and she reveled in the frenzied rush of his kiss.

The moment went on, and she lost herself in him until he lifted his head, meeting her gaze. "I need more," he said.

"Yes."

He lowered her to her feet, hooked his fingers into the waistband of her leggings and pulled her pants down, taking her underwear along with them. As she kicked them aside, he stripped off his jeans, and when she turned back, she was staring at his hard erection.

She reached out and slid a hand over the head already covered with pre-come and moaned.

"Come on, let me feel you around me." He lifted her up again and backed her against the wall as he slid her down onto his shaft.

He glided in easily thanks to her wetness, and she felt every slick inch of him as he came to rest inside her.

"Oh, God." Her entire body shuddered at the sensation of feeling him bare. "Umm, condom," she said, not really caring. This was Matt. Her everything.

"You've got nothing to worry about," he assured her.

She hadn't been concerned. Not with him. "Me neither, but I'm not on the pill." Her sex contracted around him, and this time he let out a groan.

"You're my future," he told her. "I'm good to gamble."

A wide smile tilted her lips because ... this man. I love you," she said as he began to move inside her.

"I love you, too." He punctuated the words with a deep thrust she felt everywhere.

He pumped into her over and over, her entire body reverberating with the pressure. He hit the right spot each time and she rose, riding a wave of pleasure that was sure to take her over quickly. And when he slid a hand between them and glided his fingertip over her clit, she shuddered and the sensations became too much.

"Come with me," Matt said, and his gruff voice and the hard thrust inside took her over the edge. Delicious sensations overwhelmed her and she saw bright flashes behind her eyes as she came, flooded with feeling.

Two more thrusts and he was joining her, filling her body, heart, and mind.

She returned to herself to find him staring at her, his eyes glittering, his emotions bare on his face, there for her to see.

"I'm so glad you decided to make your move," she said as he slipped out of her.

"You're mine, Harper. Even when we weren't together, you were mine."

She braced her hands on his face and kissed him. "And I always will be."

Thanks for reading! If you haven't read THE KNIGHT BROTHERS, you can get them HERE:

Take Me Again

Take Me Down

Dare Me Tonight

Want even more Carly books?

CARLY'S BOOKLIST by Series – visit:
https://www.carlyphillips.com/CPBooklist

Sign up for Carly's Newsletter:
https://www.carlyphillips.com/CPNewsletter

Join Carly's Corner on Facebook:
https://www.carlyphillips.com/CarlysCorner

Carly on Facebook:
https://www.carlyphillips.com/CPFanpage

Carly on Instagram:
https://www.carlyphillips.com/CPInstagram

Carly's Booklist

The Dare Series

Dare to Love Series
Book 1: Dare to Love (Ian & Riley)
Book 2: Dare to Desire (Alex & Madison)
Book 3: Dare to Touch (Dylan & Olivia)
Book 4: Dare to Hold (Scott & Meg)
Book 5: Dare to Rock (Avery & Grey)
Book 6: Dare to Take (Tyler & Ella)
A Very Dare Christmas – Short Story (Ian & Riley)

** Sienna Dare gets together with Ethan Knight in **The Knight Brothers** (Dare Me Tonight).*

** Jason Dare gets together with Faith in the **Sexy Series** (More Than Sexy).*

Dare NY Series (NY Dare Cousins)
Book 1: Dare to Surrender (Gabe & Isabelle)
Book 2: Dare to Submit (Decklan & Amanda)
Book 3: Dare to Seduce (Max & Lucy)

The Knight Brothers
Book 1: Take Me Again (Sebastian & Ashley)
Book 2: Take Me Down (Parker & Emily)
Book 3: Dare Me Tonight (Ethan Knight & Sienna Dare)
Novella: Take The Bride (Sierra & Ryder)
Take Me Now – Short Story (Harper & Matt)

The Sexy Series
Book 1: More Than Sexy (Jason Dare & Faith)
Book 2: Twice As Sexy (Tanner & Scarlett)
Book 3: Better Than Sexy (Landon & Vivienne)
Novella: Sexy Love (Shane & Amber)

Dare Nation
Book 1: Dare to Resist (Austin & Quinn)
Book 2: Dare to Tempt (Damon & Evie)
Book 3: Dare to Play (Jaxon & Macy)
Book 4: Dare to Stay (Brandon & Willow)
Novella: Dare to Tease (Hudson & Brianne)

* Paul Dare's sperm donor kids

Kingston Family
Book 1: Just One Night (Linc Kingston & Jordan Greene)
Book 2: Just One Scandal (Chloe Kingston & Beck Daniels)
Book 3: Just One Chance (Xander Kingston & Sasha Keaton)
Book 4: Just One Spark (Dash Kingston & Cassidy Forrester)
Just One Wish (Axel Forrester)
Book 5: Just One Dare (Aurora Kingston & Nick Dare)
Book 6: Just One Kiss

Book 7: Just One Taste
Book 8: Just Another Spark
Book 9: Just One Fling
Book 10: Just One Tease

For the most recent Carly books, visit CARLY'S BOOKLIST page
www.carlyphillips.com/CPBooklist

Other Indie Series

Billionaire Bad Boys
Book 1: Going Down Easy
Book 2: Going Down Hard
Book 3: Going Down Fast
Book 4: Going In Deep
Going Down Again – Short Story

Hot Heroes Series
Book 1: Touch You Now
Book 2: Hold You Now
Book 3: Need You Now
Book 4: Want You Now

Bodyguard Bad Boys
Book 1: Rock Me
Book 2: Tempt Me
Novella: His To Protect

For the most recent Carly books, visit CARLY'S BOOKLIST page
www.carlyphillips.com/CPBooklist

Carly's Originally Traditionally Published Books

Serendipity Series
Book 1: Serendipity
Book 2: Kismet
Book 3: Destiny
Book 4: Fated
Book 5: Karma

Serendipity's Finest Series
Book 1: Perfect Fit
Book 2: Perfect Fling
Book 3: Perfect Together
Book 4: Perfect Stranger

The Chandler Brothers
Book 1: The Bachelor
Book 2: The Playboy
Book 3: The Heartbreaker

Hot Zone
Book 1: Hot Stuff
Book 2: Hot Number
Book 3: Hot Item
Book 4: Hot Property

Costas Sisters
Book 1: Under the Boardwalk
Book 2: Summer of Love

Lucky Series
Book 1: Lucky Charm
Book 2: Lucky Break
Book 3: Lucky Streak

Bachelor Blogs
Book 1: Kiss Me if You Can
Book 2: Love Me If You Dare

Ty and Hunter
Book 1: Cross My Heart
Book 2: Sealed with a Kiss

Carly Classics (Unexpected Love)
Book 1: The Right Choice
Book 2: Perfect Partners
Book 3: Unexpected Chances
Book 4: Worthy of Love

Carly Classics (The Simply Series)
Book 1: Simply Sinful
Book 2: Simply Scandalous
Book 3: Simply Sensual
Book 4: Body Heat
Book 5: Simply Sexy

For the most recent Carly books, visit CARLY'S BOOKLIST page

www.carlyphillips.com/CPBooklist

Carly's Still Traditionally Published Books

Stand-Alone Books

Brazen

Secret Fantasy

Seduce Me

The Seduction

More Than Words Volume 7 – Compassion Can't Wait

Naughty Under the Mistletoe

Grey's Anatomy 101 Essay

For the most recent Carly books, visit CARLY'S BOOKLIST page

www.carlyphillips.com/CPBooklist

About the Author

NY Times, Wall Street Journal, and USA Today Bestseller, Carly Phillips is the queen of Alpha Heroes, at least according to The Harlequin Junkie Reviewer. Carly married her college sweetheart and lives in Purchase, NY along with her crazy dogs who are featured on her Facebook and Instagram pages. The author of over 75 romance novels, she has raised two incredible daughters and is now an empty nester. Carly's book, The Bachelor, was chosen by Kelly Ripa as her first romance club pick. Carly loves social media and interacting with her readers. Want to keep up with Carly? Sign up for her newsletter and receive TWO FREE books at www.carlyphillips.com.